INSPIRING STORIES

FOR AMAZING BOYS

A Collection of Stories about Courage,
Confidence and Friendship

Emily Green

Inspiring Stories for Amazing Boys

Emily Green

ISBN:

1st edition 2022

© 2022 Emily Green

Content

Introduction

Hey there! Do you know that you are very special? There are millions of boys in this world, but there is only one of you. You are completely unique. Always remember that!

The world has many big and small hurdles in store for you. Sometimes you might think that you can't make it. You might get very scared or doubt yourself. However, I want to tell you a secret. Everybody feels like this from time to time! Even adults. Life without hurdles and problems does not exist. Where there is good, there is also bad.

Even things that scare you or you would prefer not to do are a part of your life.

Sometimes, bad experiences can also reveal something good.

You will meet many boys in the stories in this book. Boys who didn't dare at first but then courageously conquered their fears. Boys who doubted themselves but then showed inner strength. Boys who almost gave up but then discovered their confidence and didn't give up. I am sure that you can do all of this too. But you must start believing in yourself. These stories will help you with that.

You will find a picture with an important message after each story. Feel free to color the picture. It's best to use lots of bright colors. This way, you will better remember the messages and never forget them, even in the difficult moments of your life.

Remember that you are unique, lovable and important to this world.

You are good just the way you are!

A New Adventure

Ben idly poked at his cereal. He had hardly slept last night. His excitement about today was too great. Normally, he always ate a lot at breakfast, but today Ben simply had no appetite. However, it wasn't because of the food. The six-year-old boy actually loved the cereals that his mom prepared for him every morning. He even drank only half of the large glass of orange juice that he usually liked so much.

"Aren't you going to eat a little more, sweetheart?" asked Ben's mom with concern. Ben just shrugged his shoulders and lowered his eyes. Mom put her spoon aside, stood up and went to her son.

She put her arm around his shoulder and continued in a soft voice.

"You should eat more so that you have enough energy! Today is your special day after all!"

Mom was right. Ben really did have a very exciting day ahead of him today. It was his first day at school. For weeks, Ben could think of nothing else. On the one hand, he was looking forward to soon being a schoolchild. But on the other hand, he was also afraid of this day. There was a special reason for that. Ben and his parents had recently moved from the village to the city because his mother had found a new job. Ben was not at all happy about this. He would much rather have stayed in his old village. There, he went to nursery school and knew many other children. Now that he lived in the city, he was far away from his nursery school friends and he didn't know anyone yet.

That made Ben sad. He desperately wished that he would finally make new friends at school.

Now his dad came for breakfast too.

"Good morning, my boy! Today is your first day at school. You've been waiting for this day for so long and now it's finally here. Aren't you happy?" Dad asked with a smile on his face.

He tried to cheer Ben up a little, as he could feel that his son was very excited. Ben replied in an upset tone.

"Yes, I am! Of course I'm excited. But to be honest, I feel a bit queasy. I'm sure the other children already know each other from nursery school and I'm here all alone and don't have a single friend! What if no one wants to talk to me or sit next to me?"

Ben was a boy who always expressed his worries openly and honestly. He knew he could talk to his parents about anything. "But why shouldn't you make any new friends? You're such a great boy. So if I had to go to school again, I would definitely want to sit next to you. You just have to approach the other children openly and be friendly to them. I am sure you will make lots of new friends soon," said his dad with positivity. His father's words calmed Ben down a little.

Hopefully, Dad will be right, he thought to himself.

With new courage, Ben ran into his room. There he put on his black jeans and his favorite dark blue jumper that his grandma had given him for his birthday last month. The jumper had a hood and a big tiger with its mouth open was printed on the front. Tigers were Ben's favorite animals. Then he slipped into his black and white sports shoes and picked up his school bag. It was green and had a football player kicking a ball away on it. Ben made it with his mom. As a football fan, he was very proud of his school bag.

"Ben, are you ready? We have to leave now!" his mom called out.

"Yes, I'm already dressed. I'll be right there!" replied Ben, after looking at himself and his school bag in the mirror one last time. Finally, he put his school bag on his shoulders and was ready for his first day of school.

Once they were all ready, they went to school by car. During the car ride, Ben's dad started talking.

"Oh, I still remember my first day of school. I was so excited at the time and didn't really want to go to school. But then I learned to read, do maths and write. I made so many new friends.
Someday, I'm sure you'll be grateful that you were able to go to school."
Ben listened to his dad's words and somehow, he could hardly wait to finally be there.
His dad stopped the car, and the engine fell silent.
They had arrived at school. Mom saw the big yellow building with brightly painted windows. Ben watched the many children

and parents gathering around the entrance. Some children stood together in groups where they talked and giggled. He thought to himself that these children must have been in the second or even third grade. He watched the crowd with wide eyes. Somehow, his nervousness came back. His mom lovingly took his hand, leaned over and whispered in his ear, "Come on, we're going to look for your classroom together now. It's surely the best one in the whole school!"

Mom, Dad and Ben now walked across the playground and then into the school building.

Everything seemed so big and new. The long corridors, the many colorful pictures on the wall and so many children who were all happy and chatting with each other.

His classroom was in the left wing of the school. He was glad that his parents accompanied him, because he would have had a hard time finding the classroom on his own. A tall young man with a brown beard and a book in his hand was already standing in front of the classroom.

It was Mr. Winter, Ben's class teacher. Ben already knew him from the introduction day he had attended with his parents.

Mr. Winter was already waiting at the door. He was in a good mood and said hello to everyone.

The other parents and children were gathered around him, chatting. When Mr. Winter saw Ben and his parents, he greeted them in a cheerful voice.

"Welcome. Nice to have you here."

Then he turned to Ben.

"If you want, you can already choose a seat where you would like to sit." Ben, in his excitement, could only bring a shy "yes" past his lips.

Now it was time to say goodbye to his parents. Mom gave him another quick kiss on the cheek and said, "Have a great first day at school, sweetheart."

Dad also patted Ben on the shoulder again and told him, "I'm sure you'll have fun! We'll pick you up here later."

Ben entered the classroom and let his gaze wander around the room for a moment. The blackboard already said "Welcome" in big letters. Pictures with big colorful letters and numbers were hanging on the walls.

Some children were already sitting on the chairs. There were no seats left in the first row. In the second row on the right, he saw a boy with short brown hair and a yellow T-shirt sitting alone. Should he just sit next to him? What if the boy preferred to sit alone or already had a seatmate who would join him later? Ben was getting more and more worried. Maybe he should look for another seat after all. He would have preferred to be back in the nursery school with his old friends.

But then he remembered his father's encouraging words.

Ben decided to summon up all his courage and simply approach the boy. His heart began to beat faster and faster.

"Hello! Is the seat next to you still free?" Ben asked the boy in a slightly trembling voice. "Yeah, sure, there's no one sitting here yet. You're welcome to sit next to me!" the boy replied, visibly excited.

Ben carefully put his school bag aside and put his school bag on the table. Then he sat down and said, "My name is Ben, by the way." "And I'm Thomas," the boy replied.
The two smiled at each other briefly and then started chatting about their time in nursery school and their hobbies.
Ben and Thomas understood each other immediately and quickly realized that they

had many things in common. For example, they both loved drawing pictures and playing football. In addition, tigers were also Thomas's favorite animals. Thomas also didn't know any of the other children yet and was therefore very happy that Ben had approached him. Ben's worries about not making any new friends at school were suddenly gone. With Thomas as his seatmate, he already felt much more comfortable. Who knows, maybe Thomas would even become his best friend one day? Ben could hardly wait to meet the other children in his class. Earlier, Ben would have liked to sink into a hole in the ground to hide, but now he was quite sure that he would make lots of new friends here and that he would enjoy school.

What a beautiful day!

I AM GREAT

The Poem

"Jack and Jill
Went up the hill
To fetch a pail of water,
Jack fell down
And broke his crown
And Jill came tumbling after.
Up Jack got
And home did trot
As fast as he could caper,
Went to bed
To mend his head
With vinegar and brown paper."

Luca had finally done it. Satisfied, he closed his school book. Now he knew all the lines of the poem by heart. Tomorrow, he was to recite the poem in front of the whole English class. Luca was eight years old and was now in the second grade. He had a loving mom who helped him learn the poem. He recited the poem to her over and over again at home. So far, almost always flawlessly. If he ever forgot how the poem went, his mom only had to tell him the next word and it would all come back to him. Sometimes Luca got annoyed, even if he made tiny mistakes when reciting the poem. His mom calmed him down when he did that.

"Oh, Luca, don't take

the little mistakes so much to heart. They happen to everyone. Nothing and no one in this world are perfect."

Luca realized that his mother was right. But still, he didn't want to make a single mistake. He tried so hard because he really wanted to get a good grade in this class. Next to sports, English was his best subject. He got a B in his report card last year, which he was very proud of. Of course, his mom was also proud that her son had such an excellent way with words. But she didn't really care whether he got an A, a B or any other grade on his report card. For her, the main thing was that Luca did his best and was happy.

Like every day, Mom came into Luca's room in the evening to say goodnight.

"It's almost 9 pm. Time to go to bed,

otherwise you won't get out of bed tomorrow! You want to be fit, don't you?" His mom knew, of course, that Luca was supposed to recite the poem in English class tomorrow. That's why she really wanted him to get enough sleep that night. While Luca lay in bed, he recited the poem quietly several more times from beginning to end. "Jack and Jill went up the hill to fetch a pail of water..." At some point he finally fell asleep, exhausted.

The next morning, Luca and his mom had breakfast together. A little absently, he poked around in his cereal. It wasn't that he didn't like it. Rather, it was the excitement that robbed him of his appetite.

"What's the matter, sweetheart? Why are

you so quiet?" inquired his mom.

"Oh, it's nothing," Luca replied as he looked down at the floor, slightly embarrassed.

Luca wanted to keep his fear to himself at first. But Mom knew him just too well and naturally sensed that he was upset about the poem. Mom put her hand on his shoulder and looked at him encouragingly. Then she spoke in a soft voice.

"Don't worry about the poem. You've been studying just fine."

Luca slowly raised his head. Of course he had studied, but that wasn't his point. He said sadly,

"Yes, but what if I forget something and the other children laugh at me?"

Mom immediately replied, "I can't imagine anyone in your class laughing at you. I'll let you in on a secret: your classmates are at

least as excited as you are."
Mom gave Luca a kiss on the forehead and took him lovingly in her arms.

Then, Luca packed his school things and went to school. During the first lesson he had maths class. Normally, he always listened attentively and paid close attention. However, today he found it harder than usual to focus. Because of the poem, he was just so tense and couldn't think of anything else. It was good that he had English class in the second lesson and was finally able to recite the poem.

Dinnnng rang the school bell for second period. Luca's class teacher, Mr. Bibber,

stood up and said,
"We will now recite the poem. I hope you have all studied well. Who wants to go first?"
Immediately, the whole classroom went silent. So silent, in fact, that you could have heard a pin drop. After about ten seconds of silence, which had felt more like ten minutes to Luca, Mr. Bibber continued.

"All right. If none of you want to volunteer, then I will choose someone now."
After this sentence, all the children began to avoid eye contact with Mr. Bibber in a panic. Luca stared at his table. His heart began to pound faster and faster. He did not want to be the first to recite the poem under any circumstances. In his mind he said to himself, Please not me. Please not me. Finally, Mr. Bibber spoke up.

"Luca! Please come forward and recite the poem for us."

What a bummer! thought Luca to himself. He then walked with wobbly knees from his seat to the front of the blackboard. The other children were visibly relieved not to have to recite the poem first. Now they all looked eagerly at Luca.

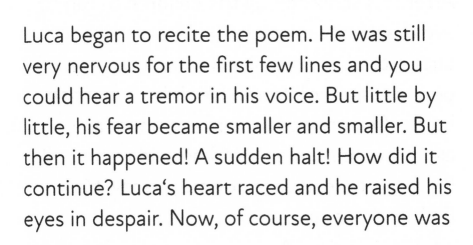

Luca began to recite the poem. He was still very nervous for the first few lines and you could hear a tremor in his voice. But little by little, his fear became smaller and smaller. But then it happened! A sudden halt! How did it continue? Luca's heart raced and he raised his eyes in despair. Now, of course, everyone was looking at him with wide eyes.

But no one laughed, just as Mom had said. Mr Bibber noticed that Luca couldn't remember how the poem went by himself.

"And broke his crown..." Mr Bibber said, hoping to help get Luca's memory back on track.

"And Jill came tumbling after!" exclaimed Luca, who fortunately now remembered immediately. Then he recited the poem completely flawlessly until the end.

"You did that very well, Luca! Thank you very much! You may sit down again!"

Slowly, all the pressure fell off Luca and he felt liberated. After the lesson, he asked Mr.

Bibber what grade he had received.
A B! Luca smiled and was just happy. How excited he had been!

And now he had finally made it and no one had laughed, although he had faltered briefly. Luca was very proud of himself because he hadn't let his fear get him down. The next poem would certainly be even easier for him. And who knows? Maybe one day he would speak in front of a lot of people and make big speeches? He also learned that it's usually not so bad if you make a mistake.

Luca couldn't wait to tell his mom everything.

I TRUST
MYSELF

Alone in the Bakery

The first rays of sunshine of the day woke Peter up on this Saturday morning. It was November and winter had finally arrived. It was cold outside and snowflakes covered the otherwise green meadows and trees. Peter had turned six last month and was now in first grade. He was a rather shy boy with black hair and brown eyes. He liked winter better than summer. He just loved to build snowmen and go sledding with his friends.

In a good mood, Peter hopped out of his bed. Still in his pajamas, he left his little bedroom and ran into the kitchen, beaming with joy. There he saw his mom preparing breakfast. She put cups and plates on the dining table.

She had also prepared a fruit tea, the smell of which slowly spread throughout the room. Mmmh, that smells delicious! thought Peter. Mom was just putting the jam jar on the table when Peter came in. He smiled briefly at Mom and greeted her as always with a friendly "Good morning, Mom" and a kiss on the cheek.

"Good morning, my sweetheart!" she replied and then continued in a slightly more serious tone.

"We have a little problem. Unfortunately, when I went shopping yesterday, I forgot to get rolls and pretzels for us. Could you please go to the bakery and get some?"

Peter replied in surprise, "But I've never been shopping alone before! Can't we go together, like always?"

Mom replied, "I'm afraid that's not possible.

Your little brother Linus has caught a cold and is now coughing terribly. He really wants me to stay with him and look after him."

Peter could understand his mom. He loved his little brother, Linus, more than anything. He was only two years old. That's why Mom really shouldn't leave him alone. Especially not when he was sick.

"All right, then I'll go alone," Peter finally said. Mom was visibly relieved and happy about his help.

"Thank you very much, Peter. Please get four rolls and three pretzels, and as a reward you may also buy a donut. You like donuts so much! I've already put the money for it in the pocket of your winter jacket. It's very kind of you to help me."

Afterwards, Peter got changed. He took off

his pajamas and dressed himself nice and warm. It was cold outside and he didn't want to catch a cold like his little brother. On the one hand, he was really looking forward to the donut. He loved donuts and they had always been his favorite food. On the other hand, doubt and fear were beginning to creep up inside him. After all, he had never been shopping alone without his mom before. What if he couldn't get a word out at all and the other people in the queue had to wait impatiently behind him? Or what if he completely forgot what he was supposed to bring with him in the first place because he was so scared? Thousands of thoughts ran through Peter's mind. However, he really wanted to make his mom proud and also be a good role model for his little brother, Linus. That's why he decided to go anyway.

"See you soon, Mom," Peter called as he zipped up his winter jacket and walked out of the warm house into the cold, snowy winter landscape, his heart pounding.

Fortunately, the way to the bakery was neither far nor dangerous. The bakery was just across the road and there was also a pedestrian crossing leading across it. Before Peter crossed the road at the crossing, he looked left and right to see if a car was coming. He had learned that from his mother. "Better safe than sorry!" Mom always said.

So to be completely sure, he looked left and right again. Still there was no car in sight. So Peter crossed the crossing and was now standing directly in front of a small blue building with the yellow glowing lettering "Bakery".
He closed his eyes briefly, took a deep breath

and hesitantly opened the door. As soon as he entered the shop, a short ring tone sounded. The ringing announced to the shop clerk that a new customer had just come in. "Good morning!" said Peter in a slightly trembling voice.

He had learned from his mom that you should always greet other people nicely, so he made every effort to do the same today. The shop clerk greeted him kindly in return and then continued to serve an elderly lady who had entered the bakery before Peter. That wasn't so hard! he thought to himself. He slipped his left hand into his trouser pocket and clenched a fist. Peter always did that when he was very excited. Then he let his eyes wander around the shop.
He saw many pretzels, rolls and even small

and large cakes. And of course there were the donuts he loved so much! After the elderly lady had paid, it was finally Peter's turn. Immediately, he became very nervous again. His heart began to pound loudly and quickly. He couldn't remember the last time he had been so excited.

"Hello! What would you like, young man?" the shop clerk asked in a friendly tone.

"Hello! I-I-I would like three rolls and four pretzels, please!" replied Peter in a shaky voice.

Then, only a few seconds later, he realized that he had mixed up the numbers.

"Sorry, I just got mixed up. Four rolls and three

pretzels, I mean!" Peter corrected himself, visibly nervous.

"Oh, that's not a problem at all. It happens to lots of customers!" the shop clerk replied sympathetically and smiled at him kindly. She had probably noticed that Peter was very excited.

"And then I'd like this donut!" said Peter, pointing with his index finger at a large donut with chocolate icing and colorful sprinkles.

"All right. That will be exactly eight dollars," said the shop clerk, putting everything into a paper bag.

Peter put a five-dollar note and three one-dollar bills on the small tray.

"Thank you and goodbye. Enjoy!" the shop clerk exclaimed.
Peter said goodbye, nodded his head slightly and left the shop.

Suddenly, a feeling of unbridled joy arose in him. He could not describe what he felt at that moment. He had just gone shopping alone for the first time in his life. Although he was so very excited and even afraid of it, Peter didn't let it get him down. He also realized that it wasn't so bad to slip up and say something wrong because that can happen to anyone. Maybe I'm not so shy after all! thought Peter.

Happy and in a good mood, he walked home again.

Once home, he could no longer suppress his smile.

"I bought everything for us, Mom. And I even really enjoyed it! If you don't mind, I'll go shopping by myself more often in the future."
Mom was overjoyed and praised her son.
"You did a great job! I am very proud of you, Peter."

By now, Peter, Linus and Mom were really hungry. They couldn't wait to finally start breakfast.

At the table, Linus, who was fortunately feeling much better, asked,
"Can I please have some of your donut?"
"Of course, I'll be happy to share it with you," Peter replied immediately.
He broke off a piece for his brother and put it on Linus's plate.
The two brothers ate the donut with relish.

Yummy!

I AM UNIQUE AND IMPORTANT TO THIS WORLD

The Basketball

Dinnng rang the bell loudly at the front door. Immediately, Max ran through the hallway with big steps and opened the door with anticipation.

"Hello! I'm glad you came!" said Max to his best friend, Tim, beaming with joy.

Max and Tim were both nine years old. They met in primary school and had been almost inseparable ever since. At school they were seat neighbors and almost every weekend the two met to spend time together. They were never bored together and always had a lot of fun.

"My mom made pancakes for us. Would you like to try them?" asked Max.

"Yes, I'd love to!" replied Tim.

They quickly ran into the kitchen. "Mhhhm! They taste especially good!" said Tim, smacking his lips. Each of them gleefully ate four whole pancakes.

After they had eaten their fill, Max and Tim went out into the garden. It was a beautiful warm summer's day in August. The sun was shining and there was hardly a cloud in the bright blue sky. The lawn in the garden was a vibrant green and the flowers were blooming in their most beautiful colors.

Max had an idea.

"We could throw a ball to each other, just like we did in PE class last week. Would you like to do that?" asked Max.

"That sounds great. I'm in!" said Tim without hesitation.

Immediately, Max ran and got his basketball from the garage. It was orange with black stripes. Max had received the ball from his mom for his birthday only last month.

Max and Tim started throwing the ball to each other. At first they stood close to each other and threw the ball slowly and carefully. But as time went by, they learned to control the ball better and better.

So they moved further and further apart and the ball flew back and forth between them higher and higher and faster and faster.

And then it happened! Tim was careless and stumbled when he tried to throw the ball to Max with a running start. The basketball flew in a high arc over the fence into the neighbor's property. There, the ball landed in the middle of a flower bed of all places! For a moment, Max and Tim looked at each other in silence.

The horror was visible on Tim's face and his cheeks turned all red. He was embarrassed to have thrown the ball into someone else's garden.
"And which one of us is going to get the ball now?" asked Tim, utterly bewildered.

"Well, you, of course. You threw the ball over. So you have to bring it back," Max answered with conviction.

"But the ball is not mine. It's yours. I think you have to get it!" Tim said angrily.

Max didn't feel like arguing with his best friend and remembered his mom's old saying: the wiser gives in.

That's why Max finally said, "All right, I'll go and get the ball."

Max stood in front of the wooden fence that separated the gardens of the two properties.

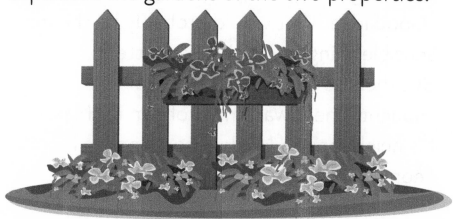

With an exasperated look on his face, he began to sigh.

"How am I supposed to get over there? The fence is so high and has sharp points. I'm afraid of hurting myself if I try to climb over. And besides, my parents have forbidden me to do that. What am I going to do?"

"Climbing over the fence would be far too dangerous. I agree with you completely. Just ring the neighbor's doorbell! Maybe he can unlock his garden gate for you and let you into his garden," Tim said.

"Good idea. That would probably be the most sensible thing to do," Max admitted.

But then he felt a little queasy at the thought. There was one problem for Max: his neighbor was Mr. Johnson, and his friend Leon was very afraid of him.

Mr. Johnson was an older man with bushy white eyebrows and a mustache. He was also almost two meters tall. He looked pretty scary to Max! And then he also had this deep, raspy voice! Max had only known Mr. Johnson by sight. The two of them had never spoken a word to each other, but Mr. Johnson had spoken to Leon's parents several times. Usually they talked about the weather or the beautifully landscaped garden.

Nervous, Max walked up to Mr. Johnson's

front door. How might he react? Will he get angry or look at me crossly? What happens if I start stuttering in fear or can't get a word out at all?

Max had a thousand thoughts running through his head, but then he gathered all his courage and rang the doorbell.

"Be right there," a deep male voice rang out, and a little later a tall man opened the front door.

Now Max was standing directly in front of Mr. Johnson, who was almost twice his size. Max's heart began to pound faster and faster. "Oh, hello, Max! What a surprise to hear you ringing my doorbell. How can I help you?" said Mr. Johnson in a friendly tone.

Max stammered. "Good day, Mr. Joh- Joh- Johnson! Sorry to disturb you, but my ball accidentally landed in your flowerbed. I'm sorry. Can I have it back, please?"

Now, standing so close to Mr. Johnson, he looked even bigger to Max than usual.

"But of course! That's no problem at all. I'll unlock the garden gate right away and then you can get your ball back. Just let me know the next time you play ball again. Then I'll open the garden gate and you can always fetch the ball when it flies in!" said Mr. Johnson with a slight smile.

Max was surprised at how nice and good-natured Mr. Johnson actually was. After Mr. Johnson had unlocked the garden gate, Max carefully retrieved the basketball from the flowerbed. Fortunately, no flowers were damaged. "Thank you and have a nice day!" Max said goodbye.

Visibly relieved and in a good mood, Max returned to Tim with the basketball in his hands. What thoughts he had had before! And how great his fear had been earlier! But then it turned out that Mr. Johnson was actually a very nice and helpful man.

Full of joy, Max and Tim continued to play.

This time, however, they kept more distance from the neighbor's property and threw the ball much more carefully than before. After all, they didn't want the ball to fly over again. Today, the two did not want to disturb Mr. Johnson anymore.

That day, Max learned an important lesson in life: he realized that the first impression of a person can also be deceptive. Just because someone looks different, or maybe even scary, doesn't mean that this person can't still be very nice. As long as he was friendly to other people and remained polite, he didn't have to be afraid of a conversation.
Max had shown a lot of courage today and he was mighty proud of that.

I AM GOOD
THE WAY I AM

A bad Grade

Eliah sat tensely in his seat. With a blank look, he pushed his pencil case around on the table. Usually Eliah was always in a good mood, but today it was different.

"Now we're going to get the maths test from last week back!" he said to his seat neighbor Daniel.

"Oh, that's right. Well, I thought the test was pretty easy!" said Daniel, who was always very good at maths and obviously couldn't wait to finally find out his grade.

Eliah, on the other hand, did not find the test easy at all. Although he had studied diligently for the test, many of the tasks had simply been too difficult for him. Therefore, he feared that he would probably not get a good grade today.

Mr. Fincher, the teacher, entered the classroom with long strides. He had a stack of papers in one hand and his shoulder bag in the other. Friendly as always, he greeted his pupils.

"Good morning! I corrected your maths tests yesterday. I will now go through the rows from front to back and give everyone back their test."

A murmur went through the classroom. Some pupils began to whisper frantically to each other. Others stared silently at the floor or chewed their fingernails in excitement.

Eliah sat next to Daniel in the second row. After a few minutes that felt like half an eternity to Eliah, Mr. Fincher had arrived at Eliah and Daniel's table. First he handed

Daniel back his test.

"Very well done," Mr. Fincher said after placing Daniel's test on the table in front of him.

"Yay, an A!" Daniel rejoiced, beaming from ear to ear.

Mr. Fincher also had a slight smile on his lips. He was happy for Daniel that he had once again scored an A.

Now, Mr. Fincher began to look in the pile of sheets for Eliah's maths test. When he found it, he stopped smiling and became more serious again. Eliah began to tremble with tension. Mr. Fincher placed the maths test on the table in front of Eliah and leaned down to him.

"I actually expected a bit more from you. What happened?" he asked in a low voice so

that the other children couldn't hear him.
Eliah looked at the red D on his maths test
and swallowed.

"I don't know exactly," he said, after a
moment's speechlessness.

He had guessed that he was worse than
usual, but he really hadn't expected this
grade. This was his worst grade so far, he had
always got B's and C's in maths.

"Well, then you must have had a bad day.
That can happen," Mr. Fincher replied.

Then he stood up straight again and went to
the next pupil.

"Oh, don't worry about it. Maybe I can help
you study in future," said Daniel, who had
overheard Eliah's grade.

"Yeah, maybe," Eliah replied, a little grumpily.
He was not at all in the mood to talk to

Daniel right now. Eliah lowered his head and looked at his table as if transfixed. He would have liked to start crying right now. But because he didn't want to cry in front of the other pupils, he held back his tears as best he could. Luckily, it was the last lesson and he could go home soon. He had never felt so sad in his life.

Dejected and sad-faced, Eliah arrived home. At lunch, his mom immediately noticed that something was wrong with him. "What's the matter, sweetie? Why are you so quiet today?" she inquired.
Eliah just shrugged his shoulders and said,
"I don't know." Then a little

later he suddenly said in a trembling voice, "I took that maths test at school last week, remember? Unfortunately, I got a D."

Because Eliah was ashamed of his grade, he actually intended to keep the matter of the D to himself. But then he realized that there was no point in hiding anything from his mom. She would find out sooner or later anyway. Mom was glad that her son was finally telling her what was on his mind.

"I don't think a bad grade is the end of the world as long as you did your best. And I know you prepared diligently for the test and have nothing to reproach yourself for. I'm sure you'll have many more opportunities to get a better grade. It's not bad," said Mom. "But it is very bad!" retorted Eliah and then said, completely distraught,

"You have to do well at school, otherwise you won't get a good job later on. As you know, I want to be a veterinarian when I grow up and you need good grades for that. Besides, I'm annoyed that Daniel always gets much better grades than I do."

Now, all the feelings he had felt in the morning at school came up again. Eliah cried and tears began to roll down his cheeks. Mom listened to him attentively and let him finish without interrupting, because she felt that Eliah needed that now.

When Eliah calmed down a little again, his mom lovingly stroked the back of his hand

and said in a soft voice, "A grade says nothing about what you can achieve in your life. If you have a dream, the most important thing is that you believe in yourself. I will always love you very much no matter what grade you bring home."

Eliah wiped away his tears, took a few deep breaths and then said,

"I love you too, Mom."

Mom hugged Eliah and then continued, "Anyone can have a bad day and not perform as well as usual. Besides, there are also many children who never get the best grades, but they still go their way and later learn a profession that makes them very happy."

His mom then paused for a moment to give Eliah a chance to digest her words.

"Do you actually know that you are very special? And perfect just the way you are.

No grade in the world will ever change that, because grades don't determine a person's worth."

Then, Mom gave him another kiss on the cheek and they continued eating.

After they had finished eating, Mom asked, "You know what, I have an idea. I want to go to the zoo with you today. Are you in?"
Mom knew that Eliah loved animals more than anything and it would quickly take his mind off things.
"Yes, I'd love to. That sounds good," Eliah answered immediately.

A little later they drove by car to the zoo. There they saw many different animals such as turtles, zebras, monkeys and even lions and elephants. During the excursion, Eliah was like a changed person and for a moment he had forgotten the incident at school.

After dinner, he went straight to bed. Much earlier than usual, because he had experienced so much today and was already tired. Lying in bed, he thought about what his mom had said. He was happy to have such a great mother. And she was proud that he was brave and had spoken openly to her about his problems. Eliah resolved from now on never to be so sad about a bad grade again. After all, there were much more important things in life.

As his mom   said at lunchtime: school grades do not determine a person's worth. Satisfied, Eliah fell asleep.

I AM LOVED

It's No Big Deal!

Steve had been getting headaches at school for weeks. When he came home today after a hard day at school, he decided to finally talk to his parents about it. As Steve was eating lunch with his parents, he finally said, "Mom, Dad, I have to tell you something. I somehow always get headaches at school. But when I'm at home on Saturday and Sunday, I always feel great. I really don't know why that is."

"Is something bothering you? Are the lessons too hard for you?" Mom asked in a worried voice.

Steve replied, "No, it's definitely not that. I keep up well in class. Yesterday I was the only child who got all the maths problems right." Dad listened attentively and now spoke up.

"Could it be that you don't get along with another child and that's why you don't feel comfortable?"

Immediately, Steve shook his head and said, "No, I get along great with the other kids and I don't have any other problems either. I don't know where these headaches come from. They come on suddenly and then I get tired."

Steve's parents were now really worried about their son. That's why they decided to go to the doctor with Steve as soon as possible. After lunch, Mom phoned Steve's paediatrician, Doctor Hoffman. Luckily, an appointment was available that afternoon. When they arrived at the doctor's office, Doctor Hoffman began to examine Steve thoroughly. He used all kinds of equipment and asked many questions, but he could not find anything either.

"Unfortunately, I can't explain why it is that Steve always gets headaches. Your boy is completely healthy!" Doctor Hoffman finally told Steve's parents.

Everyone was relieved that Steve fortunately did not have a bad illness.

When Steve and his parents were about to leave the room, Doctor Hoffman suddenly spoke up again.

"Oh yes, I have one last question. Steve, tell me, do you see everything written on the blackboard at school?"

Steve answered. "I sometimes have trouble seeing what the teacher writes on the blackboard. But if I squint my eyes tightly, I can manage."

Doctor Hoffman snapped his fingers, for now it all made sense to him. "I think now I know what your problem is. You should definitely take your son to the optician and have him checked to see if he needs glasses!" said Doctor Hoffman to Steve's mom. "All right. We will do that. Thank you very much, Dr. Hofmann," Mom replied.

They said goodbye to Doctor Hoffman and left the practice.

On the one hand, Steve was happy to have finally found out the reason for his headaches. But on the other hand he was also sad. He didn't want to get glasses under any circumstances. He was afraid of being laughed at. After all, he was one of the cool boys, and he wanted to stay that way.

"Mom, I don't want glasses. I'll just ask my teacher if I can sit in the front row from now on. Glasses are uncool!" sighed Steve in exasperation.

"But, Steve, there are really great glasses. I'm sure that together we'll find you a nice pair. Just look how many famous people and sportsmen wear glasses! We'd better go straight to the optician!" said Mom with conviction.

Steve stuck to his opinion. He just didn't want glasses. But Mom was not dissuaded and the very next day the two of them drove to the optician.

The optician was very friendly and examined Steve's eyes. It turned out that Steve could not see clearly at a distance and therefore needed glasses. In the shop there were countless glasses in all kinds of shapes and colors.

Steve tried on one pair after the other. With so many to choose from, it was hard for him to decide.

Finally, he chose a nice pair of glasses with a black frame. At home, Steve stood in front of the mirror for the rest of the day. He had put on his new glasses and looked at himself. From the left, from the right and with every conceivable grimace. Slowly, he even liked the glasses. Nevertheless, he was afraid of the next day at school. How would the other children react? After all, they only knew him without glasses.

The next day at school, Steve was very nervous. He sat down in his seat and then took the box containing the glasses out of his backpack. His neighbor Marc came and sat next to him. Steve greeted him and then said to him,

"Look what I have to wear now, Marc." Steve opened the box and showed his friend the glasses.

"It's not bad, is it? My sister and my dad have glasses too!" Marc said, quite unimpressed. Before Steve could reply, he continued, "Why don't you put them on?"

A little hesitantly, Steve put on his glasses. Marc immediately said, "Well, I think the glasses look really good on you!"

Then the lesson began. Steve was relieved that Marc didn't mind at all that he was now wearing glasses. During the break, some children seemed to notice that there was something different about Steve. Some asked if he wore glasses now. But that was all!

Nobody said anything stupid or laughed at Steve. After school, a huge load fell from his heart. How he had been afraid this morning that the other children would laugh at him because of his glasses.

After a few weeks, it had become quite normal for Steve to wear glasses. He didn't find it bad at all anymore.

And above all: his headache was finally gone!

I AM STRONG AND COURAGEOUS

Into the Water

"Wake up, Alexander! You have to get up now!" Alexander's mom called impatiently. She stood at the open door and continued. "If you keep dawdling like this, you'll be late for school."

Alexander rubbed his eyes sleepily and yawned. Then he replied a little grumpily, "It's okay, Mom, I'm getting up already."

Alexander had only been woken up by his mom's call and was still really tired. He remembered his exciting dream about a fire-breathing dragon that lived in a cave and defended valuable treasure. How he would have loved to sleep a little longer and continue dreaming.

Alexander was a cheerful boy with short dark

brown hair and big light brown eyes. Like every morning, he got dressed right after getting up and brushed his teeth thoroughly. Then he neatly folded his blue pajamas with lots of yellow stars and tidied his bed. Alexander's mom wasn't particularly strict, but she did set great store by tidiness.

Mom is right. It is important that everything is tidy and neatly in its place. That way you have more of an overview and can find your things more quickly without having to search for them for a long time, Alexander thought to himself.

For breakfast, Mom had again prepared delicious cereals with nuts and mixed fruit, which he loved to eat. While he was enjoying his cereals, he suddenly remembered that today was Friday. On this day, he always had PE class in the last period of school.

Recently, his class had started going to the swimming pool, which was located at the next crossroads near the school building. Actually, Alexander always looked forward to the sports lesson. However, since his class always went swimming, he didn't feel like it at all.

"What's wrong, sweetheart? Is something wrong?" Mom asked, a little worried. Alexander's sad gaze into space and his hunched shoulders were always a sign to his mom that something was troubling her son. Alexander hesitated briefly and then answered timidly.

"We always go swimming with the whole class on Fridays now. Today, we're even supposed to jump off the diving board into the pool."

Almost sobbing, he continued.

"Mom, I'm scared of it! Jumping from so far up into the deep water!"

"Oh Alexander!" said Mom sympathetically.
"Then just explain to Mr. Schulz that you are
afraid of heights and that's why you don't
want to jump. I'm sure he'll understand."
Mr. Schulz was really a very experienced and
mindful teacher. He was a teacher of class 3b
and taught almost all subjects. He was very
popular with his pupils, because you could
also go to him when you had problems. He
was the so-called confidant teacher of the
whole school.

Alexander now said, quite upset,
"Yes, Mr. Schulz would certainly not mind.
But the other children will surely notice that
I don't dare. What should I do if they laugh at
me or call me a coward?

And to be honest ... actually ... actually ..." he

stammered on meekly.

"Actually, I want to try jumping into the water. It must feel wonderful to fly in the air for a moment. Like a bird. But I'm just so incredibly scared of it."

Mom paused for a moment and thought about how she could help Alexander. Then she gently put her hand on Alexander's shoulder and spoke in a soft voice.

"I'm going to tell you a secret, or rather a little trick that has always helped me to overcome my fear. First you close your eyes. Then you breathe in and out deeply three times and count. Three ... two ... one ... and then you jump."

Alexander listened in fascination and then asked,
"And that really works?"

Mom lowered her head, smiled and then said, "Well, this trick has always helped me a lot. But for it to work, one more thing is incredibly important: you have to believe in yourself very firmly. As firmly as I believe in you. You can do it!"

Alexander took new courage from his mother's words. He trusted her and resolved to try the trick today.

Dinnnng rang the school bell for the fourth and last lesson. Now the time had come and physical education began. Class 3b and their teacher, Mr. Schulz, left the school building and entered the swimming hall. It was a huge hall with large glass windows. You almost thought you were outdoors because you could see the city park from the hall. Mr. Schulz said to the assembled class, "Put on your swimming clothes and then please line up in order. As I announced last week, today we will learn how to jump into the water from the diving board. I'm sure you'll really enjoy that!"

A little apprehensively, Alexander walked alongside his friend Christian to the changing rooms. Christian was his best friend. They already knew each other from nursery school and lived not far from each other. Now they went to the same class and were, of course, seat neighbors. Christian was very sporty and loved swimming. He just loved being in the water and had even been in the swimming club for some time. He first swam at the age of four and could even jump from a three-meter tower. Christian had recently told all this proudly in the playground.

"How are you? You seem so different today. Are you scared?" Christian whispered in Alexander's ear.

He had noticed, of course, that Alexander was quieter than usual and seemed tense. Normally, they chatted constantly when they saw each other. Alexander answered with his head down and his voice unsteady. "Well ... I'm already a bit excited."

A lump formed in his throat. Then he collected himself again and continued speaking.

"I've never jumped off a diving board into the water before, and actually I'm afraid of heights."

Alexander was really glad that he could talk to Christian about everything and be honest. He was his very best friend and would never laugh at him.

"Oh, you'll manage. Just don't think about it too much! I was scared too when I first jumped into the water. And now I can't get enough of it," Christian said.

After all the children had changed, they lined up behind the diving board. At that moment, the diving board seemed like the highest mountain in the world to Alexander. His legs started to shake and his face turned pale. He definitely did not want anyone to notice anything. He suddenly had the feeling that he could no longer breathe properly. Christian, who was standing in front of him, turned around briefly and tried to give his friend courage.
"You can do it. We'll do it together."
Alexander was glad to have Christian by his side now.

One pupil after the other was now to jump into the water. First it was the girls' turn. The first was Mia. She could hardly wait and jumped into the pool with a "yay". But most of the girls jumped carefully and straight as a candle into the water while holding their noses. Then it was the boys' turn. Christian was the first. He had practiced jumping into the water many hundreds of times and was happy to be able to show everyone. He jumped into the water with an impressive pike. It was actually Alexander's turn. But he hesitated and left two other boys in front of him who could hardly wait to jump into the cool water. It looked so easy for almost all of them. Most of them were laughing and really enjoying themselves.

Now it was time; it was Alexander's turn.
His heart now began to pound loudly again
and his legs felt like rubber. Nevertheless,
Alexander walked with slow, hesitant steps
to the edge of the diving board. His knees
were shaking and he actually wanted to turn
back on the spot. In the background he heard
Christian's familiar voice.

"Come, Alexander! Jump! It's easy."

At the same time, he remembered again the
secret that Mom had entrusted to him. He
took a deep breath. He exhaled deeply three
times. With each breath, his fear lessened.
Alexander closed his eyes and counted in his
mind.

Three ... two ... one ... and then he jumped. At
that moment he felt like a dolphin splashing
in the air with joy and then back into the sea.
When he dived into the water it was

unusually quiet, but immediately he wriggled his feet and came back to the surface. What an indescribable feeling it was! He had made it and was incredibly happy about it. If he hadn't dared to jump, he would never have felt this joy. Alexander was very proud of himself. Full of inner strength and confidence, he swam to the edge of the pool and climbed out of the water.

Christian welcomed him with a smile.

"I knew you could do it. It wasn't that hard!" Christian patted him on the back and Alexander realized how nice it is to have friends.

Afterwards, the children were allowed to play water polo in the water until the end of the sports lesson. Back home, Alexander could hardly wait to tell his mother about the experience. He was bubbling over with enthusiasm and pride.

"Mom, your trick really worked. I just jumped!" he told his mom with tears of joy in his eyes.

"You did a really great job. I'm so proud of you. Do you actually know how much I love you?" Mom spoke to him in a soft voice and they both hugged each other.

In the evening, when they went to bed, Mom lovingly kissed him goodnight on the forehead, as she did every day.

Then she said, "Good night. I think it's really great that you conquered your fear and didn't give up. Sleep tight, my sweetheart."

Then she turned out the light. Alexander lay awake in bed for a while tonight. He couldn't fall asleep, so troubled were his thoughts.

He had learned today that he could do almost anything if he only wanted to and believed in himself. Jumping into the water was his biggest fear and he had now overcome it. I wonder what else he will achieve?

Satisfied and happy with himself and the world, Alexander finally fell asleep.

Imprint

Please contact us if you have any questions, feedback or suggestions:
info@pisionary.com

The author is represented by: Pisionary Publishing Ltd
Adrea Omirou Ave 17, Rose Gardens Block B Apt.218
Year of publication: 2022
Responsible for printing: Amazon